HAOXIANG HAOXIANG CHI CAOMEI

I Really Want Strawberries

Written by Liu Hangyu
Translated by Phyllis Ang

I heard there are strawberries on the east side of the forest…

Who doesn't want strawberries?

Who ran ahead of me?

Everybody wants strawberries.

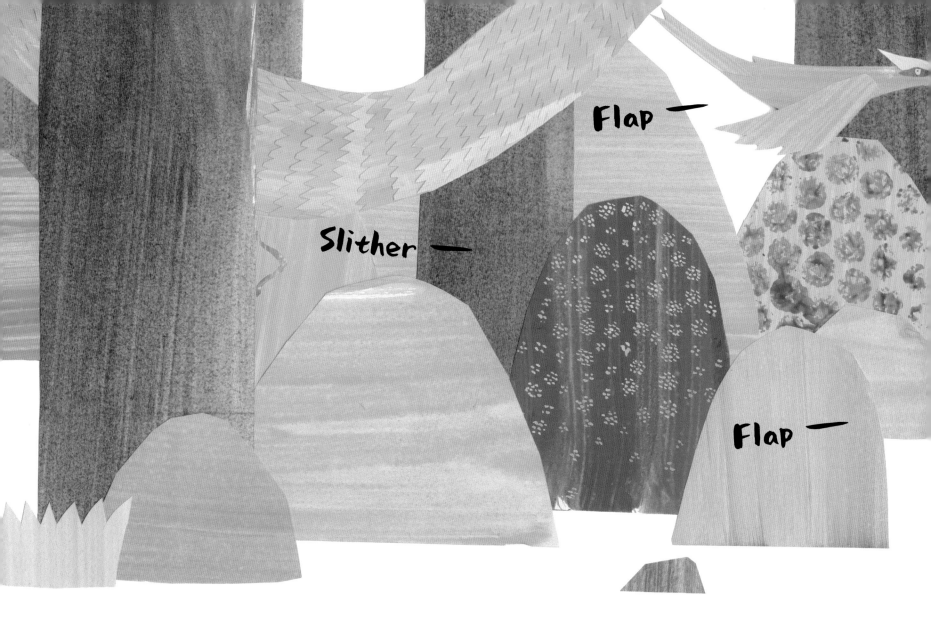

Will they be gone when I get there?

Where are the **strawberries**?

Where on earth are the
strawberries?

There are no strawberries.

No strawberries at all.

We're going home!

I still want those strawberries.

The sun is so hot.

The mountain is so high.

The night is so dark.
I really want those strawberries.

Wow, strawberries!

Strawberries are delicious!

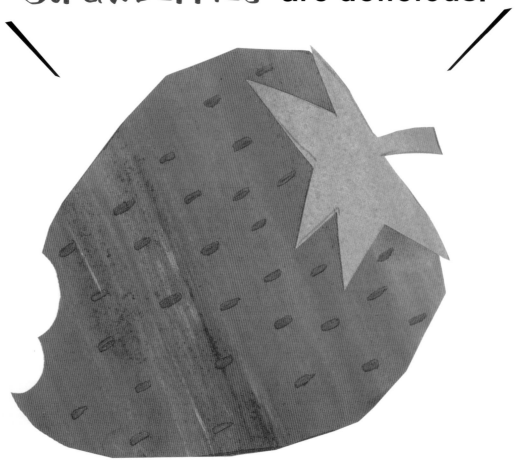

Author: Liu Hangyu

Born in 1993, Liu Hangyu is a children literature writer and a freelance artist. His short stories have been presented on magazines such as *Children's Literature, Literature and Art for Juveniles, October Youth Literature*, and *Reading Friends*, etc. He has won Bingxin Children's Literature New Works Award in 2014, Excellence Award of Reading Friends Cup Children's Literature Award (Writers Group), the 2nd Prize of 6th Zhou Zhuang Cup National Children's Literature Competition and the 2nd Bronze Sunflower Children's Novel Award. His currently published works collections are *The Lights, The Dreams*, *My Classmate is Weird*. His latest published full-length novel is *Your Feet, My Feet*. Apart from drawing watercolor pictures and making ceramic art, he has also focused on creating picture books for the past few years. *A Whale in the Sky* was shortlisted for the Xin Yi Picture Book Award. The book, *Red Fish and Bluebird*, won Great White Whale Picture Book Award (Graphic) in 2016.

I Really Want Strawberries

Written by Liu Hangyu   Translated by Phyllis Ang

Editor Jane Yang
Graphic Designer Lily Tang
Print Production Eric Lau

Chung Hwa Book Co., (Singapore) Ltd., 2021

Published by Chung Hwa Book Co., (Singapore) Ltd.
211 Henderson Road, Singapore 159552

http://www.chunghwabook.com.hk

First Published in December 2021

Printed by Elegance Printing & Book Binding Co., Ltd.

Distributed by SUP Publishing Logistics (H.K.) Ltd.

ISBN | 978-981-18-2228-5